THE BRIDGE CROSSER

By Nancy Absalonson

Illustrated by Christa Prentiss

ISBN-10: 1511753668
ISBN-13: 978-1511753661

DEDICATION

I would like to dedicate this book to my father, Steve Scheving. "Papa" taught me, through his daily actions, what a father's love truly is. His patient, kind, caring ways helped lead me to my heavenly Father's love through His son Jesus. I will always be thankful for the influence I had from my own father, and will endeavor to portray that love, as a legacy to my children and grandchildren. May the words in this book cause you, the reader, to want to live out love to your children, family, and friends daily. May the Lord's touch flow through your words and actions to those He sovereignly puts in your life, so His will eventually culminates into eternal life in His Kingdom. It's all about love!

CONTENTS

1 | HOME

Huffing and puffing until his lungs felt like they were going to explode, Tom found his legs getting heavy from running through the acres of tall green grass on his family's farm. He let himself collapse, pretending his muscles didn't work anymore. Landing on his back, with his arms flung out and his legs curved like a broken pretzel, he closed his eyes and tried to stop his mind.

It didn't work. He was too close to the sounds of his dad on the tractor, far off in the summer alfalfa field. The wind was gently blowing across the top of him, only licking the tips of the bending grass. It's soft breeze blew right over him, as if it didn't even notice he was there. Imbedded down into the smashed shape that only he could form, Tom rustled around a little. He stayed low to avoid the whistling wind, all along wondering if it was alive. "What is wind anyway?" he asked himself. It was moving, and it had a voice, he thought, but was it alive?

Just then Tom's dog barked. The faint announcement was coming from inside the two story farm house. He froze, hunkering down, purposely not responding to Scooter's call. He just wanted to be alone. Imagining his little dog wagging his tail in anxious hope of his loving owner's return, Tom wondered if Scooter's mind could picture the two of them playing and running around, or maybe just walking quietly together. He felt a little guilty hiding from him, but Scooter was so forgiving. He always trusted his master to do the right thing. Tom chose to stay and hide so he could listen to the wind. It beckoned him to get up and follow it, like his dog would follow him anywhere.

"Take me away!" he heard himself whisper.

The whisper startled him, reminding him that he was indeed alone. He sunk back into his fantasy world, spreading his arms out like an eagle, tuning out every noise but the call of the wind. It seemed to ask him to run away from his harsh world, away from the tears that stung with disappointment, away from the endless work that wearied him to exhaustion, and away from the heartache that his young life already knew.

"Oh wind, if you could only take me awaaaaaaaay...," he repeated.

Tom twisted and turned his resting body, soaring for a long time in his imaginary skies, all the while lying right there in the grass. He wanted to glide off to where there would be no fear or tension; where only kind people or no people at all were. He wondered if there was such a place to be found. Getting up, Tom kept his eyes shut, and with arms extended he decided to really follow the wind's whistle this time. The breeze's swirling sound led him first to the right, then around in a circle to the left. It kept calling in a way that Tom thought only he could hear. No one else would know how to respond. He dipped his wings one at a time, twirling and running for quite a while until something made him stop short.

Tom opened his eyes to see if anyone was there, but it was only he and the wind. Rubbing away the cobwebs from his vision, he looked more intently to see if his journey had taken him somewhere new. Reality slowly returned, but in his scan of the familiar corner, he did see something. Was this part of his daydream?

Lying before his big, brown eyes was a peculiar looking path that wound into the woods, beyond the edge of their land. His eyes followed the path, until he could not see where it kept going.

Tom noticed a wooden thing that rose

up out of the end of the path. Staring harder, he wished he could walk out to see what it was, but his fifteen minute break his mother had granted him was probably up long ago. He was most likely already in trouble for being late. Going beyond his property would bring certain wrath. Turning on his toes, he faced his place of dwelling in the distance, twisted his head back one last time to glare at the mysterious structure, then without another thought ran all the way home.

Tom's fear grew as he grew closer to his destiny. The gap slowly closed in between the unknown object and home. He could see the figure of his mother standing on the back porch with something in her hand. His blood ran cold in his sweaty body. His legs didn't want to obey, but his mind ordered them to keep moving. Where else would he go? Where else would he run? He could hear her yelling out his name with a tone that he knew all too well. Her anger made him cringe on the outside. Without realizing it, on the inside of Tom, in his very soul, he was keeping track of these unfair episodes.

The tally was larger than he thought, but with his head hung down and his heart shrinking with each new breath, he obediently returned home.

The boy's consequences for arriving late from break time were nothing new. He wasn't at all surprised to find himself lying in bed all evening, but he could never get used to the aching hunger in his belly. Going to sleep was the best escape he could think of for this plight. It always worked. He would just start dreaming about something that made him happier, and before he knew it he would fall fast asleep. Sleep never failed to rescue him from his present troubles. Sleep, like the wind, could even take away the burning pain on his backside that was trying to steal all his thoughts from him. The thrashes almost burned as much as his anger did towards his mother who put them there.

"Take me away," Tom whispered again, but this time with his teeth gritted.

He slowly drifted off to a numbing slumber, telling himself that tomorrow would be a better day. Tomorrow was

Saturday. Saturdays were always better. He still would have a lot of chores, but he also was given more free time; free time that would allow him to follow the wind's voice again.

"Tomorrow will be a better day. Tomorrow, I'll...," and he was off to sleep, under his thin, gray blanket.

2 | THE DREAM

Streaming rays of summer sunshine broke through the old curtains on Tom's bedroom window. One ray hit him right on an eyelid, making the inside of his vision so bright that he could no longer hang onto the dream he was having. He sat up, brushing the messy hair from his eyes, trying to remember all the details of his dreamland adventure. In the episode he was walking along in an unknown, wide open spot. He suddenly noticed that someone was following him. He tried to turn and look to see who it was, but each time that he turned he could only see a bright light, which hid the figure of whoever was following him.

Several times, Tom kept walking and then quickly turning, thinking that if he was fast enough he could beat the bright light and see the person. He was never faster than the light. Each time that he turned away, he heard a gentle voice saying, "Come to me."

Tom was afraid when the man spoke, though his voice was soft and comforting. He decided to run past him on one side so that he'd get beyond the glaring light. Then he might be able to find out who this mystery man was. .

"Okay", he said to himself in the dream, "On the count of three, I'll turn. One…two…," and he woke up. "Oh great, now I'll never see him," he said out loud.

He found himself yearning to know who the man was so badly, it reminded him of wanting to run back to see the wooden structure at the edge of his property.

"Never see who?" his mother called from downstairs. "Well, if you mean your father, you won't see him if you stay in bed all day long. Get up now, so you'll be at the table before breakfast is over," she said gruffly.

"Okay mother," said Tom, sweetly.

He forced his tired, still painful body to get up out of bed. During his morning routine he realized how hungry he was, so he tried to hurry through his chores before it was too late to fill his stomach. Just one more thing; he had to feed the dog.

"Good morning boy," said Tom's father, as Tom approached the kitchen table.

He was a kind enough man, though Tom didn't see him much because he worked so hard out in the two fields that they owned. His crops brought in a meager living for the family of three. Tom often wondered if his dad ever thought of him at all during the long farming days. If he did, he never said so. Tom longed to go with him to help him with his work, but his mother would have none of that. She always recounted all of the farm accidents that she knew of growing up. Tom couldn't imagine any accident hurting more than she hurt him. Even if it did hurt more, at least it would only be an accident. If only he could tell his father.

"I won't have one of mine turn into just another news story for the townspeople to talk about for years to come," his mother would say. Tom's father always went along with her so there would be no trouble.

Besides thinking about helping his father, the boy also wondered what it would be like to get to know him; to really spend time with him, asking him about his likes and dislikes, favorite color, or maybe even future dreams. Dreams? Oh there he was again, daydreaming instead of concentrating on what needed to be done.

"Good morning Father," Tom finally replied. "It's going to be a good day." Tom's spoke these words with his head down. He was trying not to let his father see the gleam in his eye.

"Oh? Why is that Tom?" his father asked.

"Well, because you'll get a lot of work done, and well…so will I," Tom replied thoughtfully. His mother gave him one of her rare smiles, thinking he'd learned his lesson from the night before. It was easy for her to justify her own actions. Tom found himself tremendously craving both of their approval. Strangely enough, he would rather taste approval than the sweet dripping syrup on the buckwheat pancakes he was about to dive into.

"Well, we will see, Tom," his father said, trying to end the conversation quickly, so he could eat in silence.

Tom shoveled down his breakfast politely, finishing even the eggs that were a little dry and burned around the edges. He wanted no trouble today! He was certain he could get his morning chores done before noon, so that he could…

"Tom," his mother called.

"Yes mother."

"I want you to go and gather all of the

chicken eggs before doing your regular chores this morning," she ordered.

"Yes mother," Tom dutifully replied, getting up to waste no time. He put his plate in the sink, pushed in his chair, and went straight out to the chicken coop, wondering all along if the added work would thwart his chances of free time that day. In fact, all morning while Tom was busy, he kept thinking of only two things; the corner path that he wanted to escape to and the man in his dream. He couldn't get them out of his mind. One called to him as much as the other. Who was the man? What was the wooden object by the path? His curiosity haunted him.

Outside, while doing his chores, something out of the corner of his eye interrupted his thoughts. It was the neighbor lady; an old woman, working in her yard hanging clothes. She was far more real than anything his mind had wandered to, lately. He did wonder, though, if she was real, because he had never been close enough to see her in detail or even hear her voice. His mother said to stay away from her. The reason for staying away had something to do with her talking to herself, all crazy like. Tom didn't mind keeping his distance because he figured that she would just be like every other adult that paid so little attention to him anyway, unless they wanted him to do something for them.

Grandpa was the only exception. When he spent time with Grandpa, he would kindly stare into Tom's face as if his grandson was the most important person on earth to him. Then, straining to hear every one of Tom's words, Grandpa would listen on the edge of his seat leaning his head back, laughing at whatever Tom said. Even if Tom barely thought it was funny, Grandpa always found pleasure in anything he said. He never asked Tom to do any favors for him. In fact, Grandpa wanted to do whatever he could for Tom. He felt special around his grandfather, but since he wouldn't see him today, why daydream about him now. Tom started getting back to accomplishing the work before him.

Echoing in the distance was his mother's voice, repeating the very idea he had just scolded himself for.

"Better not be daydreaming again, young man. Get back to work," she said predictably.

As his hands and body routinely moved, he still couldn't stop his mind from drifting. He specifically was asking himself now if the older neighbor lady was about Grandpa's age. Could they possibly know each other? There weren't many people around those parts, and Grandpa went to the same old school that Tom attended during the school year. They had to know each other, he thought. Maybe they even had a whole history together. Maybe they were related. He bet that she could tell him stories galore.

She may even be as nice to him as Grandpa was. No, that couldn't be possible. Anyway, his folks would find out if he ever snuck near her. She looked so mild, though, unable to hurt a fly.

Tom was sometimes so lonely, flies were company to him. He filed away these new questions in his mind the same way he filed away so many others, never expecting to come across any answers.

He also never expected to quit dreaming or asking himself things like, "Who was that man following me in the dream that seemed so real? What is the wooden object at the end of the path? Why do they both seem to be calling me, saying, 'Come to me'?" He wanted to know, and he wanted to go.

3 | THE BELL

Finally Tom earned his fifteen minute break. He was hoping for his usual thirty minutes, but the extra egg gathering stunted his break time. He walked slowly out into the fields so his mother wouldn't be suspicious, but as soon as he was out of her sight, he began to sprint. Tom thought he felt someone watching him during part of the flight, so he kept glancing over to his right side. He saw no one but the harmless old woman.

He knew that he was not allowed off his property at any boundary line, but the wooden structure kept luring him on. He had to know what it was. Besides, he had already rehearsed this trip in his mind. He wouldn't go any closer than he needed to. He would just carefully take a few brisk steps over the line, look at the object, and then quickly return to his own property. No one would ever know.

Right as Tom reached the corner of the field, he heard the supper bell ring. "That's odd," he said to himself. This bell usually only rang in the evening when supper was ready, unless there was an emergency. Once, when the bell rang, twin calves were being born. Another time, his mother had spilled a pot of boiling water. Some landed on her arm, scalding her badly. Tom decided to still take his few steps in swiftly to see what he could see, then run back home. He cautiously approached the object, noticing that it was some kind of bridge.

The bridge was not a normal bridge that went over water or anything. There was no water; only dry ground in this small clearing of the wooded area. All bridges he had ever seen only had one walkway. This one had two, perpendicular to each other. One walkway crossed from the side close to Tom's property out to the woods. The other walkway crossed over the first, from side to side, meeting in the middle. There were four entrances, each leading to the middle. Tom realized that it was shaped like a small t, with one arch shorter than the other. Tom, being good at math, figured the longer archway was about four times longer than him, maybe twenty feet. The other archway was possibly five feet less than the first, making it about fifteen feet long. During these brief calculations Tom noticed some sort of symbol with words written in the center of the bridge. He was totally out of time, though, so he turned to run home without getting a good look at the round symbol. He darted like a jack rabbit to find out why the bell rang. Even though he was compelled to go back home, all the while he wished he had more time at the bridge.

The way home felt longer than usual because of the constant ringing of the bell. It became alarming to him! It usually only took about five minutes to run the length of this smaller field. As he arrived on the back porch of his home, he could hear voices inside. One was his mother's and one was unfamiliar to him. He opened the door to go in, still trembling and gasping for breath from the run. He came into the living room to find the older neighbor lady standing in the doorway with a look of terror on her face.

"There's been a terrible accident," her feeble voice said, full of concern.

Tom's mother was scrambling to get a sheet out of the linen closet, as if she were going to hang it on the line. Tom was confused. His mother quickly grabbed him by the arm, pulling him through the house to the front door, but then remembered that she should dial the operator to contact Dr. Tashion. She frantically turned the crank on the phone which was on the wall.

"Hello, Operator. Get me Dr. Tashion, and make it snappy," she barked.

Tom vaguely heard something about a farm machinery accident. She just kept repeating, "You have to get here as fast as you can!" Then she ended with, "No more questions! Just get here before he bleeds to death!"

Slamming down the receiver, Tom's mother quickly grabbed him by the arm again, pulling him out the front door, but then stopped in her tracks once more.

She turned from the winded boy and looked desperately to the woman for help.

"I'll show you where he is,' said the woman, calmly.

Tom didn't want to run anymore, but he figured the older lady couldn't be too fast herself. He was somewhat surprised to see what adrenaline could do for all three of them. He had never seen his mother run before, but she shot out faster than any of them, looking back for directions from the pointing neighbor a couple of times. After his mother reached the crest of a slowly inclining hill, Tom could hear her gasp and pick up her pace. She had seen the halted tractor and knew her husband was close.

Within another two minutes she was arriving at the scene of the accident. Shortly afterwards, Tom joined his mother kneeling beside his fallen father.

Behind him he could faintly hear the old woman saying, "Don't touch him. Leave him for the doctor. Don't move him. He'll be alright. He's going to be in good hands. He's in good hands," she repeated. Tom wondered if she meant the doctor's hands. Why did she say he was going to be alright? Who's hands could he be in that would make him okay? Maybe she was crazy, like his mother had always told him.

4 | COME

They couldn't believe their eyes when they first saw the sight. There Father was, about a half a mile away from their house, right in the middle of the alfalfa field. On the ground Henry, Tom's father, was groaning in pain, grabbing one flattened leg. He was still talking, but deliriously.

"Jumped off the tractor. Couldn't see. Tractor. The tractor moved. Hit me. My leg, my leg," Henry said in anguish and groaning.

Tom's mother clumsily wrapped strips of sheet around the leg, above the break, to try and stop the bleeding. The break was so bad in one spot that they could see bone protruding out of the skin.

Dr. Tashion had come so quickly that within moments of the older woman's arrival on the scene, he was racing toward their direction in his car, right through the field. Tom wanted to do something to help, so he took the red scarf off his father's farm hat and started waving it in the air frantically.

"Over here. We're over here," he cried.

The big car was now heading right towards their side of the tractor. The Dr. jumped out of his car, with his black doctor's bag, and ran to the bleeding man. He briskly took Tom's mother's place, adjusting the sheet and adding his own new tourniquet, then removing hers.

She was hysterical, asking, "Did I do

alright? Is he going to be okay? Tell me, tell me!"

Dr. Tashion tried to back her away from Henry, not wanting her frantic behavior to rile up the already traumatized patient.

"If you're going to ride with me to the hospital Tilda, you're going to have to calm down," the physician said firmly.

Tom shuddered to hear, for the first time, a person that would talk with such authority to his mother. He was amazed to also hear her first name, Matilda, only pronounced as Tilda. I guess this is a small town, thought Tom to himself.

"Okay, I will, I will," said the scared woman. "I just have to go with you. Please don't leave me here alone. Don't leave me alone."

"Alright, then, come now," said the doctor, as he picked up Tom's father by reaching underneath each arm from behind and gently dragging the hurt man to the car. Dr. Tashion had put a board for a splint attached to the wounded leg, so it was stabilized for the loading and unloading that was necessary to transfer him to the hospital.

As the car drove off, it took a few moments for Tom and the woman to notice that they were the only ones left out there in the field, standing next to the tractor that had caused all of this. They stood there stunned. Frozen, they watched the car drive away.

"You stupid tractor. You caused the accident! I hate you," yelled Tom, kicking the huge tire, without even realizing how loud and angry he sounded.

"Come with me, child," said the gentle lady.

When Tom heard her words, for a split second they took him back to his dream. He was staring now at the speeding car, watching his father leave in the direction of the sun, while simultaneously trying to see the hidden man in the light again. He blinked and looked toward the only face that was there. Her eyes were full of compassion, beckoning him to come. Echoing in his ears were the words, "Come to me."

"Are you hungry boy?" asked the kind

hearted soul.

Tom's father was the only one that called him boy. He tried, but he just couldn't seem to get any words out of his throat. He swallowed and it felt like there was a big marble stuck there, aching and making him want to cry. Instead of speaking past this lump, he just let go and began to sob.

Instinctively the woman held out her arms and Tom didn't resist. "There, there, boy. It'll be alright. You'll see," said the woman. "You'll see. Your father's in good hands."

"But it's not fair," said Tom, and the flood behind the lump in his throat broke loose. "I wanted to be with my father. Why did the accident even happen? Why couldn't it have just happened to her…I mean…to someone else? Why?" He cried uncontrollably for quite some time while the woman simply held him. She understood that it was what he needed. She also understood why Tom wished the accident had happened to his mother, so she never said a word about that to him.

It dawned on Tom, while crying in her

arms, that he had never experienced this before; seeking comfort in anyone's embrace. He had often wondered what it would feel like. He had seen other kids do it. He knew what just a brief hug felt like, but not a reassuring, safe hold to linger in. This woman, as a stranger, comforted him in a way that he had never known. This "crazy one", the one that had watched him from a distance for so many years, made him feel more at peace than his own mother ever had. Tom felt guilty and didn't know why. He was confused.

After a long time of tapering down his tears, Tom slowly pulled away from the neighbor, leaving wet blotches on her apron. When he didn't know what else to do, she gently picked up his hanging chin and said, "Follow me."

5 | FOLLOW

The woman slowly led him to her house. They were both still numb from the incident, walking in a daze. The entrance to her home was inviting, with hanging plants and flowers.

As Tom entered her main room he

motioned to the couch with a look that said without words, "May I?" Sinking down into her soft, worn cushions, Tom couldn't figure out why he felt more at home in this never before seen house than in his own. It was as if he had known her for a very long time.

She offered him some biscuits and honey, with some wild berries in a bowl of sweet cream. He didn't think that he should eat while his father was going through a life or death emergency, but the aroma of the food soon swayed his doubts.

"Come and move in here by the radio, son," the woman suggested.

Tom followed her like a little puppy. He sat down at the table to listen. There was a story hour being broadcasted on the one station they received out in those parts of the countryside. To Tom's surprise he soon found his eyes as heavy as his heart felt. His mind wanted to stay awake, because rarely would he be allowed to listen to a show like this at home.

"What if mother doesn't know where I am?" he silently began to ask himself.

"What if father dies and I don't find out? What if this nice old lady suddenly shows her true character and becomes like the old woman in Hansel and Gretel? What if…," and he drifted off to sleep, with his head slumped over his arm on her table.

While the man's voice on the radio droned on, Tom began to dream a second time about a different man; the man he had dreamt of before. He still couldn't see his face. The rays of light were even brighter now. Tom thought he might be closer to him this time. Instead of finding a way to trick the light man into catching a glimpse of his face, Tom was too worn out to run. He decided to just lay there and listen to his voice. Maybe he would say his name. Sure enough, he began to speak.

"Follow Me," was his summoning.

When Tom heard that sweet voice again, strangely he wanted to leave everything and follow him. Instead, he woke up with a start to another voice. He couldn't remember where he was for a moment, until his neighbor's head peeked around the corner to check on him. Her tender eyes gave him the same feeling he had just had in the dream. Reality soon crept back into his brain, again, to remind him of the whole horrible day, with his father's accident.

"Bad dream?" she asked, in a grandmotherly tone.

Tom, still not willing to talk, shook his head no. As the day wore on, they passed the time trying to put together a thousand piece puzzle. Words were unneeded, so it remained quiet and peaceful in the midst of the turmoil that spun inside of Tom's mind and heart. He wondered why his new companion didn't seem to carry the same fears he did. She never brought up the accident. She acted so relaxed. The phone rang, breaking the silence.

"Hello," answered the woman. "Yes, I understand. Okay then, I will," she replied. Hanging up the phone, she explained to Tom that his father would have to stay in the hospital for a few days. He had lost a lot of blood and the doctors wanted to monitor him for a while.

"Is he going to die?" asked Tom.

"Well Tom, now you know it's too early

to say what will happen, but your father is in good hands." said the woman again. "You can stay here with me until your mother gets home," she said, reaching out to the boy one more time, with his bottom lip quivering.

Tom began to feel the crying coming on again. He was imagining all the terrible things that could happen to his father. They might have to cut his leg off. He could die, in spite of what his neighbor said. He might not be able to farm ever again, and then how would they get any money for food? Tom just kept thinking up all the worst possible scenarios, and no amount of soothing that his neighbor could offer would take away the pain he had inside. Even though Tom wasn't close to his father, he loved him. He felt safe with him. He looked up to him. He wanted to be like him in many ways.

Tom stepped away before his neighbor could hold him, and gave her a look of desperation. As if she knew what he needed, she said, "Go on, boy. Follow your heart."

This response puzzled him. What did she mean? She couldn't know that all he wanted to do at that moment was to run to his father's closet and grab something of his to hold. Why did she say, "Follow", just like in his recent dream? He turned and ran home.

When he arrived at the closet, he found one of his father's favorite shirts. He crumbled to the ground and went into a fetal position, clinging to it and smelling it. He knew that the woman had followed him home. He didn't mind her presence. He didn't care who saw him or heard him right now. Scooter crawled up next to Tom, licking his face. Why is it that a dog knows when you need comforting?

"Oh God!" he cried, clutching Scooter.

All he wanted was to have his father back. If he thought his life was hard before, what would it be like without his father? Tom wondered if there even was a God. If so, why would he listen to a little boy, let alone answer his request? He couldn't stay still. He began to run, again, past the woman. He saw her nod in approval, as if she knew what he was doing. How could she know, when he didn't even know himself?

The boy decided to go out to the corner of his property to see if his neighbor would follow. She must be way too tired, he thought. Even though he was exhausted also, he started out. Nearly halfway there, Tom turned to see if the woman was behind him. Remarkably, in the distance, she followed at a slow steady pace.

If his mother stayed at the hospital, Tom thought to himself, maybe the lady would stay with him at his house. She did invite him to stay at her house overnight. He might like that. If his mother got a ride home right now, and found both houses empty upon arrival though, she may lose control of her temper again. Should he be doing his chores? Tom decided that no matter what the consequences, he was determined to continue running to the bridge.

6 | WORDS

When Tom arrived at the corner he felt nervous, but not from his neighbor's gaze that he saw over his shoulder. The nervousness was from a lack of understanding what this place was, and why it had a strange effect on him. He had to find out what drew him there. His new friend kept her distance, giving him space to explore. He sensed that she gave him freedom to roam at the same time as keeping an eye on him. He laughed at himself to think that he felt comforted by an old lady. What could she do if anything bad happened?

Tom stepped slowly past their property line, knowing that his mother would flip out if she could see him now. He continued to follow the short path, not wanting to be disobedient to her wishes on one hand, but on the other hand needing to find out why the wind had brought him here. He could tell by now that his neighbor knew exactly what he was doing and coaxed him on with her hand signals.

Cautiously, Tom stepped up onto the first board of the bridge. Looking back once again, he saw the woman smiling. He kept going on up the curved walkway until he reached the very middle of the big cross shaped bridge. Yes, he could see it very clearly now. The whole bridge was in the shape of a cross.

Tom looked down at the inscription in

the middle, under the symbol. He saw what appeared to be three short sentences. The first and third sentences had three words, while the second one had only two. The problem was that it was not written in English. Tom imagined some ancient tribesmen centuries ago building and painting this awesome thing.

"How can I ever find out what these words mean?" he asked himself out loud.

The woman remained quiet, sitting a short distance away on a stump. Tom walked over all four of the arms of the cross bridge. He even walked around it on the ground. He thought it was strange that someone would build a bridge that may never be found or used for anything. It didn't lead to anything.

What if the words are a clue that tells whoever the finder is where to go next, he wondered? Somehow Tom imagined himself as the discoverer, maybe even the owner of this bridge. He felt important on it, like he belonged there. He could tell as he looked more closely that it was handmade. The wood was not fancy as he had seen from some manufacturers. Who was the builder, he asked himself?

Just then his internal questions were interrupted by his external follower. Surprisingly the older neighbor walked right up onto the bridge like it was on old favorite fort or something. She grinned when she looked at the emblem, as if she could read it.

Tom asked, “You know about this?”

She nodded, yes.

“Do you know what this says?” Tom asked with interested eyes.

Once again, she nodded yes.

7 | SIMON

After a long silence, Tom's neighbor motioned for him to sit on the edge of the bridge. She sat down first, turning her head to the left and pointing to her home. The distance startled Tom. It was much closer than he imagined. He began to realize that this structure was actually on her property. Tom sat down for the revealing of the secret. She simply opened up her mouth and began to talk about her husband.

"His name was Simon," she said in remembrance.

She sighed, resting her forehead on one hand.

Tom asked, "What happened to him? I mean, did he know about this bridge? Could he read the message?"

"Eleven years ago, when you were still a baby, Tom, Simon was alive," the wise story teller explained. "He was my husband. The good Lord never gave us any children of our own, which grieved Simon something fierce. Why, when you came into this world he used to pick you up and smile all over, as if you were one of his own. Your mother didn't take too kindly to strangers holding her only son and all, but your father stood between Simon and her, letting him hold you all he wanted. 'Don't steal pleasure from an old man.' he would say to her.

One day, his weakened arms slipped a

little, while he was picking you up. You fell a short ways to the ground." said the woman. She gently reached up to Tom's forehead and lightly touched a small scar above his left eyebrow.

He followed her touch with his own curious, responding fingers. "So that's how I got that."

She continued, "Simon was horrified to see the blood coming out of your head. He raced you to your mother, holding his handkerchief over the wound. From that day forward, neither one of us were welcome anywhere near your house. Your mother made such a big fuss about it that your father would have been fighting his live long days if he hadn't given in to her demands," she said in a disgusted voice.

"But what does all this have to do with the bridge?" asked Tom.

The woman patiently replied, "I'm getting to that. Simon was a praying man, Tom. He had dreams."

"Dreams?" inquired Tom, sitting up straighter.

"Yes and those dreams matched the

words in a book that was Simon's favorite," the woman recounted.

"What book" asked Tom? "Does it have these words in it?" pointing to the bridge.

She rose ever so slowly, from the day's fatigue, and sauntered around the clearing in the woods to choose her own words carefully. "I'll show you the book when we get back to my place, boy. You have to understand, Tom, that there was a man teaching my Simon this special message."

"What man" asked Tom? "Can I meet him? Is he still alive," he begged to know.

"Slow down, son," the patient teacher chuckled. "You always did have inquisitive eyes. I can see that your mind is right behind them. Tom, the man lived over 1,900 years ago. He is in the book I'll show you. This book is from God. Simon, after hearing about God's man and his message in this book, started to read in the book daily. He was so touched by this message that he meditated on it every day.

These letters look like English, but they are really Icelandic. Simon only wrote in his native language when he wanted to make a strong point. He also spoke Icelandic when he was fired up about something. He prayed about what part of the book to write on the bridge for a long time until one day he announced that he was going to build it. You see, Tom, I always let him do whatever his fancy was. I found joy in just sitting back and watching how God led him. Sometimes, while he was working out here, I'd bring him food and drink so the poor man wouldn't die of starvation or thirst during his task. He would just say, 'Man cannot live by bread alone, but by every word that proceeds out of the mouth of God.' He was quoting the man in the book, named Jesus."

"I've heard of Jesus before, from my Grandfather," said Tom.

"It took months for the old geezer to build the bridge," the woman kept talking and smiling. "He finally explained to me that it was all for you, Tom," she relayed gingerly.

"For me?" asked Tom, furrowing his brow with confusion.

"Yes child. Simon felt that from the

moment he laid eyes on you, The Lord God in heaven told him that he would be the one to tell you about your heavenly Father, not your earthly father. You see, Tom, Your heavenly Father had only one son, like your daddy did. He decided to send him to earth to become like us, so that he could show us how to get to heaven. My Simon wanted to be the one to tell you all about this son, Jesus. It broke Simon's heart terribly when he was banned from seeing you, but he trusted God for a way to still relay this message to you. This is it," she said pointing to the bridge.

"But I don't understand," Tom said. "Who is this Jesus? The only thing my Grandfather has told me is that some day when I'm old enough to be out on my own, he would tell me more about him."

"Well, honey, I don't like talking against your mother and all, but she doesn't allow that name spoken in her home, or around you," replied the woman, gently. "That just goes to show you that people either love or hate Jesus. Simon loved him, and wanted you to love him too. This bridge is the way he chose to tell you. And as for your grandfather, he should've told you by now."

"Ma'am, I've just got to know what those words say," begged Tom.

8 | ABIDE

The elderly woman was finally ready to disclose the secret message.

"The first three words on the emblem say, 'Come to Me'," she said.

Tom gasped as he heard the very same words that the man hidden by the shining light in his dream had said.

"The second two words say, 'Follow Me'," she continued.

Tom dropped his jaw, putting one hand over his mouth, as he heard her speak the words from his second dream. "I don't believe you. You've been spying on me."

The woman continued on, pretending that she didn't even hear Tom. "And the last three words say 'Abide in Me'." She sat back with such a relief that it looked to Tom as though she had been holding that secret for an eternity. He wondered about so many things at once, that to wonder what eternity was didn't even seem strange at this point. Then he wondered if he should tell her of the dreams. How could it be that she said the words that only he heard in his dreams? Could it have been this Jesus in his dreams? Would Jesus visit him again with the third line? There was so much to ask; so much to learn.

"What does this Jesus want with me?" he asked out loud, trying not to sound too confused.

"He wants to help you, Tom. He has seen your pain. He has heard your cries. He wants to save you from your sins, and heal you on the inside," she answered knowingly.

"Heal?" asked Tom. "Can this man, this Son of God, or whatever he is, heal my father's leg? Because if he can, I'd go wherever we'd have to, to find him and bring him to my father."

"He is very capable of doing just what you are asking for, Tom, but you don't have to go anywhere to find Him. He is right here with us now."

Tom looked around in the woods to see if someone was hiding there. Someone surrounded by light.

"No, boy, His Spirit is here. You can't see Him. He is like the wind. You can feel him and you know He is there, but you can't see Him."

"Did you just say wind?" asked Tom. "You were watching me in the wind, weren't you?"

"No, Tom, but I did say wind. Jesus is here as sure as the wind is. His presence is here. His Spirit is here. He lived on this earth a long time ago, performing many miracles to show people that He was God's Son and that He loved them. He explained that if we follow the way He lived, and come to Him to talk, which is called prayer, that He would show us where His Father God was, so we could go there too, to be with Him. He will take us there to live with Him forever. But most people didn't believe Him. In fact, some rulers of the land hated Him so much that they wanted Him to die. They captured Him, questioned Him, accused Him of crimes He did not commit, then nailed Him to a wooden cross to hang and die."

"A cross," Tom said quietly, as he stood up and looked at the shape of the bridge again.

The puzzle pieces in his mind were starting to come together; the reasons why he was so drawn to the bridge, his dreams, the neighbor's embrace, his wanting to escape his life, and wanting to run to get away; maybe to run to Jesus. With all the running he'd been doing, maybe he needed only run to this cross; to the bridge. Maybe the bridge did have a message for him, Tom thought. How could a story about someone dying help him now?

She continued, "The good news, Tom, is that three days after Jesus died on the cross, God made Him rise up from the grave. He was alive a little while longer, until He had told His friends what to do and what was going to happen. Later, He floated up into the clouds to be with His Father in heaven. Now, the Holy Spirit is here, so we can still hear from Him. My boy, if you want to talk to Jesus, He is right here."

Tom looked down, nervously, saying, "I don't think He'd want to talk to me."

"Tom, God knows all your thoughts and actions before you say or do them, but because of what Jesus did on the cross, you can be forgiven. God wants to give you a brand new start."

"Does Jesus control the wind?" asked Tom.

"He sure does, sweetheart," she replied.

"What does abide mean?" Tom continued in his usual habit of questioning, as he looked down at the bridge words.

"Abide means to live with. He wants to

be with you all the time, Tom. He wants to live, or abide in your everyday life."

Tom thought back to the way he felt after entering her home for the first time; the safe feeling he knew on the bridge, the way he felt when he heard the voice of the man in the dream. Was this because Jesus was in those three places?

"Do you want to know how to live in Him, child?" she carefully prodded.

A flood of emotions hit Tom's soul, along with a hundred more questions. He had to go to this Jesus for his father's sake, but could He really trust Him? He wanted to always know that same warmth and love that he had found. It must be true, he told himself, but what if this woman is crazy? What if this is all just a story?

Doubt began to swirl one way in his mind, with the desire to follow Jesus swirling the opposite direction. What if he was just lost in imagination again? What if this was not real? He went over the events in his mind again, trying to make sense of them. There were too many coincidences; the dreams, the words on the bridge, his empty feeling without God, his desperate need for Him, Simon's work and love for him. Everything seemed to be pointing towards Tom answering this Jesus, and coming to Him.

"I have to," said Tom. "He might help my dad. I want to know how I find Him." Suddenly Tom stopped and said, "Wait! I can't go to be with him, --- unless --- well, He knows what I've done wrong. He wouldn't want me with Him. I'm a bad boy sometimes. Do you think He could fix that, Ma'am?" Tom asked with shame.

"Child, I don't think He could, I know He can," she replied. "Close your eyes and forget about everything around you. Only concentrate on Him dying for us sinners, like you and me."

Tom did as she suggested, even though he couldn't imagine her sinning.

9 | PRAYER

Tom closed his eyes and began to think about how much power it would take to change things. How could anyone make a mangled leg work again? How could anyone make his family problems go away? Those thoughts made him lay back on the cross bridge, sighing.

He began to tell God and the woman all the things he could think of that he, Tom, had chosen to do wrong. There was the time he had thrown a pumpkin on someone's property, and then run away. And the time he snuck cookies up to his bedroom when he wasn't supposed to be eating. But the worst of all was how he felt about his mother. Tom spilled out years of anger toward her, trying to sort out what was so unfair about the way she treated him, but admitting the guilt of how he hated her in his heart for what she had done.

When he was empty of words and sins, he opened his eyes and noticed that he had rolled right onto the middle of the bridge, face down, with his arms outstretched as if he were hugging it. He looked up at his neighbor and didn't know what to do with the emptiness.

"Just tell Him, son."

"Dear God, I have told You about me, but now I want to know about You. I don't think you need anybody like me, but I sure need You. Can You help my daddy? Can You help his leg? If you do, I would do anything for You. Well, I don't know anything I could do for You, but I would try," he prayed.

All of a sudden, the emptiness began to slowly be filled up with joy inside. He thought he even felt better than when he was with his grandfather. He felt lighter than a feather that could blow in the wind. The more he talked to God, he felt like a new person inside. It seemed like he could face anything, all of a sudden. He felt sparkly; more clean than when he took long baths in the winter. He felt cleared of all that wrong he told God about. "Wow!" he exclaimed. A smile broke across Tom's face as sure as the sadness that was there before.

Daytime was turning to night. In that sweet dusk, the old woman decided to tell Tom her own name.

"Tom, I want you to call me Nanna. My real name is Hannah Olson, but I've always dreamed of someone calling me Grandma. Your mother wouldn't likely hear of that, so let's keep it at Nanna, since it's close to my name"

This time it was Tom who opened his

arms to her for a hug. "Nanna."

She suggested that they walk to her house for the night, explaining that his mother had asked for him to stay with her so she could remain at the hospital overnight.

"I like your house," said Tom, shyly.

"OK now. I suppose we could just get you ready at your house after lunch tomorrow, to go see your Father in the hospital."

"Tomorrow?" Tom asked with his mind churning again.

Somehow he didn't mind waiting for tomorrow. After all, Nanna had to wait all those years to talk to him and tell him of the words on the bridge. He admired that. And, if Jesus really could help him, he should be happy to wait for tomorrow. He wondered if Jesus makes all tomorrows? He could feel something different inside. Was it the man in the light? Was it Jesus, coming to live in him? Why should he be worried about tomorrow? They walked away, Tom turning to look at the bridge about every third step, until he couldn't see it anymore.

10 | THE TRIP

Nanna's couch proved to be quite comfortable for a bed. As morning's light drifted in through the sitting room's curtains, Tom had no trouble rising. As he got up on this beautiful Sunday morning, Tom was bounding with zeal and energy. He had enough steam to carry him through all the extra chores that he remembered he did not do the day before. He felt like he could do anything, just as long as this Jesus could help his dad.

Entering the kitchen, he said, "Morning Nanna," as if he'd known her all of his life. "I'm off to get all the chores done so we can go to the hospital."

"Now wait a minute Tom. Those chores can wait. It's Sunday, the Lord's Day today, and He would have you just relax, instead of working. Do you ever get a day off?"

"Well, no Ma'am, I don't. But I have to at least feed the animals. Even God would want me to do that," he said smiling.

"Have you asked Him?" inquired Nanna.

"I haven't, Nanna, but...." then he stopped to go back to the couch and to pray. As he tried to talk to God, he also talked to Jesus. Then he listened to see if He would talk back. He noticed that when he was quiet, he could feel the same sensation in his chest as he did when the man in his dream had spoken to him. It was the same feeling as when he tried to listen and follow the wind. He got up to tell

Nanna.

"I think He's trying to tell me not to be afraid about today. I think he knows I am afraid," said Tom.

"That was Him, Tom. The way you can tell it's Him is when His voice brings peace that you can't explain, inside your soul," Nanna said.

"You mean right here?" Tom asked, pointing to his chest.

"Right there. You can also tell it's Him when you find those same words in the Bible. That's what you call confirmation."

"The Bible?" asked Tom.

"Yes, the Bible. It's the book I was telling you about yesterday. It's God's word to us. Here it is," said Nanna, reaching to the book shelf behind the couch.

"May I read this whole book?" asked Tom.

"Of course you can, Tom, but you should know that it will take you at least a year to get through it. Much of it is stories of long ago, all true, of men and women that followed God before Jesus came. That part of the book is called the Old

Testament. Then the New Testament, right here, is filled with stories of when Jesus lived, and also stories of some of the first Christians that followed Him after His death and resurrection."

"Christians?" asked Tom.

"Yes, boy. That is a name that is given to every follower of Jesus. It means one who is like Christ. Jesus Christ."

"Was that His last name? Christ?"

"I think you can look at it that way, Tom. Jesus' name means the one who came to save; the Messiah."

"Wow! There is so much I don't know. I'm not sure I can learn all of this stuff."

"You will, son. You have your whole life ahead of you, and the help of the One inside of you. You have a long time. You can read and learn about getting to know Jesus, and His Father, God, and the Holy Spirit, who now lives in you, from now on. Just take it a day at a time."

"Maybe most of the chores can wait," said Tom. "I'll just go and feed the animals, after I read some in the New Testament about Jesus."

So Tom sat down and read many words, such as these:

Matthew 1:21 - "And she shall bring forth a son, and thou shalt call his name Jesus; for he shall save his people from their sins."

Matthew 4:19 - "And he saith unto them, 'Follow me, and I will make you fishers of men.'"

Matthew 11:28-30 - "Come unto me, all ye that labour and are heavy laden, and I will give you rest. Take my yoke upon you, and learn of me; for I am meek and lowly in heart: and ye shall find rest unto your souls. For my yoke is easy, and my burden is light."

And many other scriptures were written in Tom's heart, as he read them on the pages of the book of Matthew, that morning. One thing bothered him though. He could not find the words, "Abide in Me", so he asked Nanna.

"I'll read John 15:4 to you." The wrinkled old fingers thumbed through the familiar pages and stopped at this passage; "Abide in me, and I in you. As the branch cannot bear fruit of itself, except it abide in the vine; no more can ye, except ye abide in me."

11 | GOOD NEWS

Tom's grandfather arrived in his truck soon after lunch. It hit Tom that he had been so wrapped up in the events of the last two days that he had forgotten his manners. He didn't know what to introduce Nanna as, so he just said, "Grandpa, I'd like you to meet Mrs. Simon

Olson."

"It's a pleasure to see you again, Arlo," replied the woman, reaching for his hand in a familiar way.

"And you too, Hannah," Grandpa replied.

"Arlo? Hannah? I knew it. I just knew you two knew each other," said Tom, knowing he'd eventually hear stories of how, later.

The drive to the hospital seemed to take forever.

"I wonder what forever will be like," Tom accidentally said out loud. He saw Nanna put her hand up to her mouth, giggling about how her new convert talked to himself, just like she had been accused of for years.

"It won't be as boring as this drive, boy, if you're wondering about that," said Grandpa. "I heard there are colors that you've never seen before, and streets of pure gold."

"Tell me some stories, Grandpa and Nanna." And they did. Eventually arriving at the hospital, Tom couldn't wait to see his father. The building was huge. Tom wondered at how small his father seemed in this large structure, yet how big he was in Tom's life. He longed to tell his father everything about his new Father in Heaven, and how Jesus could help them.

They entered the room where Tom's father lay. Tom was afraid to imagine what his father's leg looked like under the clean white hospital sheet and blanket. He practically leapt to the other side of his bed. He fell into his father's embrace like he had never done before. The love that Tom contained now was spilling over onto his dad.

"I have good news, Dad," Tom spit out. His plan to tell him privately vanished when he saw his father. He didn't mean to call him dad. It just slipped out. Not even his mother corrected him this time, though the name dad had never been allowed in their home. The name father was expected, to show respect at all times. Tom's mother looked like she had been up all night and was too fatigued to even lift her head off her hand.

"A man came to me and showed me how to help your leg," Tom explained.

"My son, we have to leave that up to the doctors," his dad replied.

"No, father, this man is more powerful than doctors. He knows more too. You've got to believe me, father. I can prove it. He came to me in two dreams, and He is here right now. Can't you feel Him?"

"I don't see any man in here, Tom, besides you, grandpa and myself," his father said bewildered.

"Dad, father, it's Jesus," Tom blurted out. "I talked to Him. I prayed for your leg. He said to not be afraid. Mrs. Olson taught me how to pray, and I just know God is going to help us," he said, with his excitement obviously building. "I just know it!"

"Well, I'll take whatever help I can get right now, son," said his father weakly, drifting off from the pain medication.

When the doctor came in from behind a plastic curtain, everyone could tell that he had been standing there for a while, before he entered. "Well let's just see about how this Jesus works," he said with a hopeful smile, winking at the two elderly visitors. "We need the Great Physician's help," he added from under his breath as he lifted the covers from Tom's father's leg. The farmer stayed asleep for a while, but as the physician unwound the very last part of the bandage on the damaged limb, everyone, including the patient, sat up anxiously looking. "Take it easy there Henry, you're going to have to go slow now, for a long time. It's going to take a lot of hard work from all of you to get through this."

The last layer of gauze came off as a broad grin came onto the doc's face. "That's just the color I wanted to see. Looks like God listens after all. Your leg is going to be just fine," he informed them. "The only long term prescription that I'm going to order is for you, Henry, not to walk at all for at least a month. Then it'll take another month, after I visit you, before you'll be working. You all will have to make sure that he gets one more thing that's very important for the healing process."

"What's that, Doctor?" asked Tom.

"Love. A lot of love. Now Tilda, I want you to listen to me very carefully," continued Dr. Tashion.

"I don't need no advice from you bout love, John," said Tom's mother.

"I said, Tilda, listen up. I know you had a hard life growing up, and you blame your father for all that, but this is now, and I am ordering you, for the sake of Henry, to put the past behind you. I want you to treat the boy and your husband with care. Do you hear me? Doctor's orders!"

"Well, I'll be! You don't have the right to tell me what to do---"

And the doctor, with authority, interrupted, "It is not only I who says this to you, but the Lord would agree!"

"Well, it'll be over my coffin that all of you with all your God talk and Jesus talk will tell me what to do. Only one person has ever really taken care of me, and that is me," said Matilda, defiantly.

Dr. Tashion turned to Tom and Arlo and said, "Don't give up on her boys. She'll take a while longer to come around, if at all." And he exited with that remark.

12 | AN END WITH A BEGINNING

For two more hours, Tom's dad dozed on and off, along with his mother, while Mrs. Olson and Grandpa continued to catch up. Tom sat transfixed as they recounted more old stories of school days and even beyond. He laughed when they laughed. He was serious when they were serious. They had not only known each other, they were very good friends, up until Tom's mother had banned Mr. and Mrs. Olson from the farm. For the past eleven years they had not had a chance to catch up, since the only time Grandpa would've seen her is at the house.

They talked of days when Grandpa and Simon used to go fishing together. Grandpa would always tease Simon about the way he even ate the meat from the fish head, after cooking it. They also shared their faith and the courage that life took during hard times. In fact, Grandpa acted a little bit like Tom had felt the night before when he wanted God to forgive him. He admitted that he didn't really think about God enough, or talk to him as he should, but for Tom and Henry's sake, he was going to do better.

As it neared time to leave, Tom got up and stood by the window of the hospital room. He looked up into the clouds and began to think about the two dreams he had dreamt before. He was thinking about how the two messages in the dreams were, "Come to Me.", and "Follow Me." He began to see the most wonderful vision ever. This same Jesus, who had been following him in the light, was now up in the clouds with His arms outstretched. Tom could see him in broad daylight. Behind Jesus were marvelous mansions located on streets of pure gold, shining in his rays. He called to Tom and said, "Come, abide in me." At the same time that the Lord asked Tom to live in him, he pointed behind Tom, back to earth. Tom turned to look at what Jesus pointed to and he saw his mother and father. Tom wanted only to float up to be with this newfound Lord, where he would be really loved. He knew that he had to stay. For the first time in his young life, he began to feel important. He might be the one to bring the good news about God to his family, just as Simon and Nanna had brought it to him.

Tom blinked and looked to the clouds to see normal clouds where the vision had once been. He turned to see the empty eyes of his mother. He then knew why he had to stay. He silently asked God what to do at that moment. His natural instinct was to reach out and hug her. He laid his head on her resistant shoulder and kissed her on the cheek. She pushed him away and said, "Stop that nonsense. Have you gone loco?"

Though Tom was slightly offended, he was determined to show her the same love that he was shown. If it took the rest of his life to win over his mom and dad, so be it. He glanced over at his Grandpa, his Nanna, and then at his dad to find all three of them smiling at him, as if to say, "We approve." He wasn't alone anymore.

On the way home that afternoon, Tom's imagination took over again. He thought of a time in the future when he could walk his father out to the bridge to show him the cross. He would have to be patient, waiting for him to be able to walk again. Tom knew that life was not going to be instantly easy. There would be extra work at the farm, finding someone to help with the fields, dealing with the wrath of his mother, and helping to care for his father's needs. He couldn't help but stay optimistic, though. After all, He had a constant companion, and it wasn't Scooter. His friend, Jesus, would now guide him through whatever he had to face. He was sure of it. If Jesus could face the cross, Tom with Jesus could face anything, and strangely, he didn't mind waiting for it to happen.

Tom's mother, after the trauma faded, began to allow Tom to have brief visits with Mrs. Olson. "Read me some more," Tom would ask Nanna. He would much rather hear her read, and add a lot of her own understanding along with the stories, then to read by himself and constantly be asking her questions. He did go back and read over what she had read sometimes, though. Some of his favorite passages were these:

Revelation 1:8 - "I am Alpha and Omega, the beginning and the ending, saith the Lord, which is, and which was, and which is to come, the Almighty."

John 14:6 - "Jesus saith unto him, I am the way, the truth, and the life: no man cometh unto the Father, but by me."

John 5:24 - "Verily, verily, I say unto you, he that heareth my word and believeth on him that sent me, hath everlasting life, and shall not come into condemnation; but is passed from death unto life."

And some days, you could find Tom out on the bridge, listening to the wind. He never expected it to take him to another discovery, but he loved pretending that he was flying away, to be up in the heavens. You could sometimes hear Tom, while he swirled with the wind, repeating some of the words he had heard from God's book. He didn't repeat them exactly the same way that they were written in the Bible. He repeated the truth in words that fit his own way of talking. The older he got, and the more he repeated these words to himself, the more he understood.

He would say: "I am Tom, a child of God. I am a follower of Jesus Christ, who will never leave me or abandon me. I will live in the mansions of the Lord forever, some day. I have come to you, Lord, and I will follow you, Lord, and I will abide in you. You took away my fear, my loneliness. You are the living bridge, who has made a way for me to cross over from earth to heaven, from death to life. Amen."

ABOUT THE AUTHOR

Nancy Absalonson was born in Seattle, Washington in 1957, and now lives in Spokane, Washington with her husband Gary. She has four grown children and six grandchildren. Nancy is currently a teacher of Special needs students in Music and PE. She has worked with children her entire adult life, teaching various elementary grades, working in church camps, leading music for Vacation Bible Schools, assisting Children's Directors, then becoming one, and staying actively involved in a multitude of organizations linked to the schools her own children went to.

Nancy attended the University of Washington, majoring in English and graduating with her K-12 teacher's certificate. She did extended studies for an additional year and a half. She now enjoys traveling, bowling, biking, spending time with family and close friends, church activities, and updating her lesson plans for her students. She is a well-respected teacher both in the public schools and in classes at her church. Nancy has been a Christian since she was fifteen.

Made in the USA
San Bernardino, CA
28 February 2016